For Anna
—S.S.

To Mum, Dad, and his
delicious vegetable soup
—J.D.

tiger tales
an imprint of ME Media, LLC
202 Old Ridgefield Road, Wilton, CT 06897
First published in the United States 2007
Originally published in Great Britain 2006
by Little Tiger Press
an imprint of Magi Publications
Text copyright © 2006 Steve Smallman
Illustrations copyright © 2006 Joelle Dreidemy
CIP Data is available
ISBN-13: 978-1-58925-067-3
ISBN-10: 1-58925-067-2
Printed in Belgium
1 3 5 7 9 10 8 6 4 2

THE LAMB WHO CAME FOR DINNER

by Steve Smallman   Illustrated by Joelle Dreidemy

tiger tales

"Vegetable soup AGAIN!"
moaned the old wolf. "Oh, I wish
I had a little lamb. I could make
a stew, my favorite!"
    Just then...

KNOCK!
KNOCK!

It was a little lamb. "Can I come in?" the little lamb asked. "Yes, my dear, do come in. You're just in time for dinner!" said the old wolf, snickering.

The little lamb was
shivering with cold.
BRRRR! BRRRR!
"GOODNESS GRACIOUS ME!"
said the old wolf. "I can't eat
a lamb that's frozen. I HATE
frozen food!"
So he put her next to the
fire to thaw.

The old wolf looked up a
recipe for lamb stew.
Mmmmmm! He felt hungry
at the thought of it.

The lamb was feeling hungry,
too. Her tummy rumbled.
RUMBLE! RUMBLE!
"GOODNESS GRACIOUS ME!"
said the old wolf. "I can't eat a
lamb with a rumbling tummy.
I might get indigestion!"

So he gave the lamb a carrot.

"Stuffing," he
said to himself.

The little lamb gobbled
down the carrot so quickly
that she got the hiccups!

HIC,
HIC,
HICCUP!

"GOODNESS GRACIOUS
ME!" said the old wolf. "I can't
eat a lamb with hiccups!
I might catch them, too!"
But he didn't know how
to cure hiccups.

He tried throwing the lamb up into the air.

HIC!

That didn't work.

He held her upside down.

HIC!

That didn't work.

So the old wolf patted her back with his big hairy paw.

The lamb stopped hiccuping, snuggled under the old wolf's chin, and fell fast asleep. The old wolf felt funny. He'd never been hugged by his dinner before, and suddenly he didn't feel so hungry after all.

The little lamb snored gently in his ear. SNORE! SNORE!

"Goodness gracious me!" whispered the old wolf. "I can't eat a lamb that's snoring!"

The old wolf sat down by the fire, the little lamb warm on his chest, and thought how very long it had been since anyone had given him a hug.

He sniffed, then sniffed again. The little lamb smelled so . . . so . . . DELICIOUS!

"Oh!" groaned the wolf. "If I eat her quickly, it'll be all right." And he was just about to gobble her up when . . .

she woke up and gave
him a great big kiss.

SMACK!

"NOOO!!!"

howled the wolf. "THAT'S
NOT FAIR! I am a big, bad
WOLF and you are ... stew!"

"Sue!" said the little lamb,
giggling. Then she pointed
at the old wolf and said,
"Woof!"

"Oh, give me strength!"
groaned the old wolf. "You'll
have to go!"

He gave the lamb a warm
sweater and put her outside.

"NOW GO AWAY!"

he shouted. "If you stay here,
I'll eat you, and then we'll
both be sorry!" He shut the
door with a **BANG!**

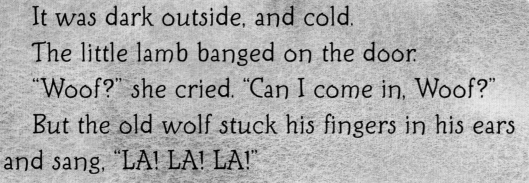

It was dark outside, and cold.
The little lamb banged on the door.
"Woof?" she cried. "Can I come in, Woof?"
But the old wolf stuck his fingers in his ears
and sang, "LA! LA! LA!"
At last, all was quiet. "Thank goodness she's
gone!" thought the wolf. "She's not safe here with
a hungry old wolf like me."

Then he thought of the lamb,
all alone in the dark woods.

"She might get lost!"

"She might get frozen!"

"She might get eaten!"

"OH NO, WHAT HAVE I DONE?"

he howled. He leaped up
and opened the door.
The lamb was gone.

The old wolf rushed out into the dark
woods, crying, "Little lamb! Little lamb!
Come back! I won't eat you. . . . I promise!"

Much, much later, a sad, soggy
old wolf trudged wearily back
to his cottage alone.

There, by the fire, sat the little lamb!

"YOU CAME BACK!" said the wolf. "Don't you have anywhere else to go?"

The little lamb shook her head.

"Er...er...then would you like to stay here...with me?" asked the wolf.

"Not eat me, Woof, no?" the lamb said.

"GOODNESS GRACIOUS ME!" said the old wolf. "I can't eat a lamb who needs me! I might get heartburn!"

The little lamb smiled and threw herself into the old wolf's arms.

"Are you feeling hungry, Sue?" asked the wolf.

"How about some vegetable soup?
It's my favorite!"